BALLET BROWN

BELLEN WOODARD

DANCING WITH ♥ HEART ♥

ILLUSTRATED BY
FANNY LIEM

SCHOLASTIC INC.

This book is dedicated to my mom and dad, whose unconditional love and discernment guide me to think critically, take academic and creative risks, and live purposefully. Thank you for never missing a moment to make sure I feel whole, represented, and valued in the dance world and way, way beyond. Love you to the moon and back a million times+.

♥BELLEN

© 2025 More than Peach, LLC. All rights reserved.

More than Peach, Ballet Brown, More than Peach Project, Crayon Activist, and Bellen are protected trademarks of More than Peach, LLC.

All rights reserved. Published by Scholastic Inc., *Publishers since 1920.* SCHOLASTIC and associated logos are trademarks and/or registered trademarks of Scholastic Inc.

The publisher does not have any control over and does not assume any responsibility for author or third-party websites or their content.

No part of this publication may be reproduced, stored in a retrieval system, or transmitted in any form or by any means, electronic, mechanical, photocopying, recording, or otherwise, or used to train any artificial intelligence technologies, without written permission of the publisher. For information regarding permission, write to Scholastic Inc., Attention: Permissions Department, 557 Broadway, New York, NY 10012.

ISBN 978-1-5461-3407-7

10 9 8 7 6 5 4 3 2 1   25 26 27 28 29

Printed in China 62

First printing 2025

All photos provided by the Woodard Family

Written by Bellen Woodard
Illustrated by Fanny Liem
Book design by Salena Mahina

INTRODUCING A WHOLE NEW VIEW OF BALLET

I wrote *Ballet Brown* for all young people, hoping that when it reaches you, it encourages you to stand as only you can.

As CEO and founder of More than Peach, my goal is, and has always been, to foster empathy, creativity, and youth leadership for the benefit of every single kid. We shouldn't settle for anything less.

You've heard of ballet pink . . . and now meet ballet brown. And it's so much more than brown shoes and tights. As young people, we're whole—and growing—and together we're helping build authentically safe spaces and best lives. Let's keep making our spaces and the world better. Definitely here for it!

♡ BELLEN ♡

I've been in love with dance since I was two years old.

To me, dance is a conversation with the world.

My ballet world was once full of color.
But then the rainbow vanished. Pink became the priority.

Pink leotard.
Pink tights.
Pink ballet shoes.

Ballet is a dance that can reflect our many beautiful stories.

I practiced, twirled and leaped,

and waited for the reflection staring back at me to express mine.

My studio's dress code said all the girls had to wear pink. So I did.

And pinned, tucked, and pulled my afro into the bun that was best for me.

I pushed my way through every jeté, chaîné, and piqué across the studio floor and stage. With every new move, I loved ballet more.

But something wasn't right.
When I saw myself in the mirror, it looked like my legs didn't belong with me.

I began to read all about ballet. Why did ballet and the dress code feel like something was missing? Where did my rainbow go?

And I found the secret! "Ballet pink" was chosen to be an extension of the ballerina, to appear as beautiful skin gliding across the stage.

"Mom, do you know why all ballerinas wear pink?" I asked. "When ballet started in Europe, the colors blended with the dancers in ballet companies at the time."

"After companies included dancers with a beautiful mix of skin tones, they never changed the dress code."

"Even now... we all know ballet pink. But no one ever says ballet brown," I continued.

"What do you think about that?" Mom responded.

"This tradition needs an upgrade," I said to my mom, "and not when I'm older or a prima ballerina. It needs to change now."

"I agree," Mom replied. "Want to go shopping tomorrow?"

If ballet didn't want to budge on its own, I'd have to give it a nudge to make more space.

The next day, I went to a local boutique. "Excuse me, do you have brown ballet slippers?" I asked.

"No, only pink. Would you like a pair?"

"No, thank you..."

But there was a better boutique out there.
"I think I found my right fit!"

"Yes, it looks great!" the boutique owner replied.

"Every ballerina should look like they are ready to fly across the stage. Just like I do in ballet brown!" I said with a smile.

I felt ready. Was my studio ready for me?

I felt great in my new tights and shoes.
Like it was meant to be exactly this way.

But not everyone understood.

"Pink is tradition," the owner said.

"Traditions should grow just like we do," I persisted.

"To start, have you considered updating the dress code?" my mom asked.

"If you don't show the ballerinas that the dress code has changed, they won't know to ask about it," I pointed out to my teacher.

But I never saw much change at the studio.

"Is this enough for you, Bellen?" my mom asked.

"No. We ALL deserve better," I said.

Dance had always brought me so much joy. I just knew that something better was waiting.

I couldn't wait to find a right-fit studio that welcomed all of me.

And that's when I learned that sometimes the most powerful thing you can do is walk away.

We walked into a new studio a little nervous but with lots of hope. We were met with bright smiles and open hearts.

The teacher answered all my questions. We knew that this time would be different.

The air in the new studio was vibrant, warm, and welcoming. And it reminded me just how much my vision was worth.

Even if I was the only one wearing brown,
I knew there would be more to come.

And just like that, I started to see the rainbow that I'd remembered from when I started ballet.

"Look!" one dancer said. "I told my mom about you and she took me shopping to find my right fit, too."

"I can finally wear my new hairstyle!" another dancer said.

I cheered for both my friends, "Looks amazing!"

"Feels amazing," they replied.

I had finally found a place that would join hands and duet with me. A place where self-expression, like the coolest crayons, colored the room.

There was nothing more magical than dancing with a full heart.

The *pointe* is—we soar when we know we're more than peach. We're each.
Find your right fit and dance as only you can.

MEET BELLEN WOODARD

Bellen Woodard, the now fourteen-year-old CEO of More than Peach and creator of Bellen's More than Peach Project (est. spring 2019), embodies entrepreneurship for a new generation. Celebrated also as the world's first Crayon Activist and pioneer of "skin-color" crayons, she has transformed whole industries with her product development, compassionate leadership, and advocacy with an aim to "let kids be kids and give them their best options."

Bellen made history as one of the youngest owners to have her products on the shelf at Target. She is a TIME Kid of the Year Honoree, among Scholastic's "most inspirational kids," a TIME100 Voices, and has been featured in dozens of top-media outlets around the world. She has also collaborated with notable changemakers including Dr. Mae Jemison, First Lady Michelle Obama, Lupita Nyong'o, Oprah Winfrey, Kelly Clarkson, Ruby Bridges, Dr. Miguel Cardona, Drew Barrymore, and many others, and her crayons have been added to museums around the world!

Bellen enjoys travel, dance, writing, world history, hanging out with friends, and spending time with family. In addition to her mom, dad, and four big brothers Quan, Qualan, Qye, and Qavi, she has two dogs she adores, a phantom goldendoodle and a beagle mix.

To learn more about More than Peach, connect with Bellen, or grab your very own products, visit www.MoreThanPeach.com.

THAT'S ME!

BALLET BROWN

I introduced ballet brown to stand for a range of colors, fill voids, and help build splendid spaces for all. Ballet brown joins hands with ballet pink as a call to action to celebrate the authenticity of all dancers, affirm the advocacy of dancers and families, applaud healthy spaces, and erase deficits. It's so much more than brown tights and shoes: It's a worldview.

WHY BALLET PINK?

Pink has always been one of my favorite colors, so as a little girl, I loved the idea of a pink costume. But in ballet, the day-to-day pink tights and shoes are not costumes and are intended to blend in with the dancer, not stand out. Many years ago, ballet pink was carefully chosen in Europe as an extension of the dancer to elevate the individual dancer's gracefulness. Yet, even as we've added brown options in tights and shoes for dancers with brown skin tones, many still view pink as the default shade of ballet. It's often the only color mentioned by name in dress codes, policy, and dance communications and is often the unspoken preference of studios. When young dancers walk into studios for the very first time, pink is always present, while brown is far more obscure. Today, pink tights and shoes are still great options for some, just not for all.

A Conversation With Studio Owners, Instructors, and Dance Families

Looking back at photos, I see that I've been wearing brown ballet slippers, brown tights, and curly, dance-friendly hair styles since very early in my dance journey. I didn't think much of it at the time. I just did it.

I've been told everything from "not wearing pink breaks the line" to "of course, you can wear brown." And I've also been told my choices were fine with the studio, when really the preference was the opposite. I've heard suggestions for dancers with tighter curls to straighten their hair and for dancers with shorter hair to wear extensions for "better" buns or ponytails.

BUT HERE'S A TIP: Brown arms and brown legs deserve the richness of brown tights and shoes, the same that's always been evident for pink and lighter skin tones. And being your best in any group starts with you being your best for *you*.

NO NEED TO BE A PRINCIPAL BALLERINA

You don't have to be a principal ballerina with a huge platform to stand ten toes down! You might be surprised at who's listening and learning from you because only *you* can do what you do. You'll see!

LOVE NOTE TO STUDIOS:

Studios, please don't leave it up to dance families to ask for what should readily be offered.

Be transparent about options and why. Support and encourage your dancers, help them celebrate their healthy choices, and ensure the support you give is immersive. Being the only one or having a different need can be uncomfortable, especially for young dancers. Review your handbooks, dress codes, and outreach materials to ensure that they are a reflection of your dancers and our world. And definitely join me in giving parity to ballet brown and making it part of your everyday.

Extra special thanks to Ms. Neo, Ms. Kathy, Ms. Elizabeth, and Ms. Megan for being the first to welcome me into my studio home, as well as Mr. Chris, Ms. Geralyn, Mr. Tomás, and the DAL dance family!

REACHING EN POINTE

Wearing pointe shoes for the very first time is a big deal for dancers, and like most, I was very excited about the accomplishment and couldn't wait to be fitted for my first pair! I hadn't considered my shoes being in any other shade than brown, and once fitted, things seemed to be moving right along. Then I learned that while the pink options were readily available, the brown ones weren't, and in my case, required ordering. But fingers and toes crossed, I looked forward to having them in six weeks, which would be just in time for a new dance season at a welcoming new studio. But my shoes were a no-show, arriving a full seven months later—and a shoe size too small.

The boutique owner casually suggested I buy a pink pair, take them home, and "pancake" them, which is coloring the shoes with either makeup or another solution. The idea of pancaking was born out of the trailblazing actions and activism of the Dance Theatre of Harlem, where dancers were encouraged to customize their own tights and shoes to blend with their skin tones. Since then, courageous and self-aware dancers have committed to doing so, even when it wasn't the most popular thing to do.

So, also determined to have my right-fit, and decades after the strides of the Dance Theatre of Harlem in the 1970s, I pancaked my very first pair of pointe shoes. It's not the easiest process for beginners and when pancaking my first pair, I actually ruined them. This put a damper on my first pointe shoe experience as my friends and fellow dancers were finding the experience overwhelmingly positive and less expensive, with ready access to their perfect shoe. But I'm happy to report that I eventually got the shoes I needed, and the next time I returned to the same boutique, my right-fit shoes (and brown ribbon and thread) were waiting for me.

Pointes to Apply for Kids & Families

1. Own Your Amazing.
You arrived that way!

2. Be a Dance Partner.
Ask about the studio culture and the commitment to everyone there. Welcome new, healthy friendships and always be open to new challenges and opportunities. Stay curious!

3. Hold Your Partner Accountable.
Expect to be represented in the literature, website, and dress code. It's not only important but lots of fun to see yourself and your friends in the studio portraits, music selections, outreach, hair textures, hairstyles, and dance roles. You're each a special part of the same dance family! If something's missing, ask for what's missing by name!

4. Own the Experience.
Dancers don't have to dream of being a professional dancer to deserve to have an amazing time. Whatever your goals are around dance, have fun!

5. Weigh Your Options. You Always Have Them.
As you move through any space, always consider the options given. Were these made with all in mind? Are your best options included? Here's your chance to talk about it. If you ever doubt any space is the right one for you, talk it over with your family and don't be afraid to consider other options. Call or visit other studios if and when you feel that way. It can be very empowering. Explore!

6. Sometimes the Most Powerful Thing You Can Do Is Walk Away . . .
A good studio is willing to learn and grow and is worth finding. A fresh start can be scary at first, but it gets easier. Thanks to all teachers, studios, kids, and families dancing with heart! I'm rooting for you!

7. Celebrate Your Right Fit!
You find your place and your people! Keep living your best life!